Cave-In at Mason's Mine

Cave-In at Mason's Mine

BESSIE HOLLAND HECK

Illustrated by
Charles Robinson

Charles Scribner's Sons
New York

to David Jack, my grandson

Library of Congress Cataloging in Publication Data

Heck, Bessie Holland.
Cave-in at Mason's mine.

SUMMARY: Young Joey demonstrates courage and a better memory than anyone thought he had when he is called upon to rescue his father caught in a mine cave-in during a hiking trip.
[1. Fathers and sons—Fiction. 2. Hiking—Fiction]
I. Robinson, Charles, 1931– II. Title.
PZ7.H353Cav. [Fic] 80-18637
ISBN 0-684-16718-2

1 3 5 7 9 11 13 15 17 19 QD/C 20 18 16 14 12 10 8 6 4 2

Printed in the United States of America

CHAPTER 1

Joey sat on the edge of the back seat of the station wagon watching the mountains come closer and closer. They were on vacation, and Dad was driving fast. He had promised to take Joey to see Mason's mine in the Rockies.

"I wish I had my compass," Joey said. He was a Cub Scout, but without his compass he could not tell north from south.

"You mean you lost your Boy Scout compass?" Dad asked.

"I don't think I lost it," Joey said. "I put it somewhere, but I can't remember where."

Mom turned and smiled at him, saying, "Maybe we should call you Joey I-Can't-Remember, instead of Joey Johnson."

"Mom, it isn't funny!" Joey fell back on the seat, feeling hot tears behind his eyelids. He just knew he would get lost in the mountains without his compass.

Joey had lived all his life on the plains where he could see for miles and miles in every direction. The Rocky Mountains, he knew from pictures in books and from watching television, were covered with trees. You could

not see far in any direction with trees all around you. Last summer, he had been lost for hours in deep woods when his Cub Scout den had gone hiking along Red River. He still trembled a little every time he remembered that day.

"Old man Mason's mine," Joey said to himself as he lay in the back seat looking up at the station wagon's dome light. He had never been inside a mine. He thought it must be awfully dark and scary inside one. And since Mason's mine hadn't been worked for years and years, maybe bears and other animals lived in it by now. On the other hand, maybe he and Dad would find some real gold.

Joey sat up and was surprised to see how much closer they had come to the mountains.

"I brought my project kit," he said, "so I'd have something to do if it rains. I want to earn a lot of Cub Scout achievements this summer."

"What all did you bring?" Dad asked over his shoulder.

"I brought a piece of rope," Joey said, "so I can practice making knots. And some road maps to study, and an airplane kit, and some puzzles, and a racer kit . . ."

"Dear me," Mom said. "You must think we're going to have a lot of rainy days. If you do all those things you won't even have time to look at the mountains, much less go hiking in them."

"I just wish I had my compass," Joey said.

"I wouldn't worry about it too much," Dad said. "You already know how to use it, and that's the important thing."

"But, Dad, I don't know north from south without it." Joey didn't say he was afraid he'd get lost without it.

"But, son, you have a good compass in your head," Dad said. "Just watch where you're going, and fix things in your mind real well, and you'll always know where you are."

Joey's shoulders drooped. Nobody understood how important his compass was to him.

Dad turned off the interstate onto a two-lane highway, then soon he turned off the highway onto a gravel road. They were in the mountains. Joey looked and looked.

"How much farther to the cabin?" Joey asked when they had driven a long way on the dusty gravel road.

"Would you believe we're here?" Dad said, suddenly turning off the gravel road into a bumpy lane that led to a log cabin. He opened the door and got out of the station wagon. Mom got out on the other side.

"Well, Joey, what are you waiting for?" Dad said. "This is it. Come on." He went to open the cabin door.

Joey climbed out of the station wagon, his project box under his arm. There was a high mountain in front of the cabin and a high mountain behind the cabin, and both were covered with trees and underbrush so thick that he could not see far in any direction. He looked

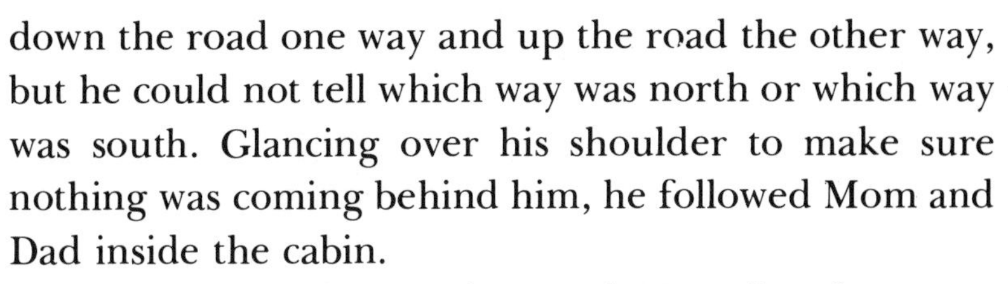

down the road one way and up the road the other way, but he could not tell which way was north or which way was south. Glancing over his shoulder to make sure nothing was coming behind him, he followed Mom and Dad inside the cabin.

It was late in the evening, and Mom lit a kerosene lamp and started supper. Joey helped Dad carry things in from the station wagon.

CHAPTER 2

Joey felt dressed up in his blue Cub Scout uniform and new hiking boots. He and Dad strapped on their backpacks. Joey was carrying the bacon and apples and cookies. Dad was carrying the skillet and forks and plates.

"Do you think we'll find any gold in Mason's mine?" Joey asked.

"I doubt it," Dad said. "Old man Mason abandoned his mine many years ago. Let's see." Dad cocked his head to one side. "I was eighteen years old, just twice your age, when your grandpa and I came up here on a hunting trip and accidentally discovered the mine. We learned later that it had been abandoned a year or two earlier. Come to think of it, it may be all caved in by now."

"I hope not," Joey said. "I've never seen inside a mine." He thought it must be scary inside a dark mine. He asked, "Dad, will we hike far enough for me to earn my achievement?"

"This hike will be plenty long for you to earn your achievement," Dad said, slapping his hat on his head. "Are we ready?"

"We're ready." Joey ran out the back door of the cabin and took a deep breath of the cool, pine-scented air. The trees were so thick that the whole world looked green.

"Hold it right there," Mom called. "I want to get a picture of this." She waited till Dad came and stood beside Joey. Then she took a shot with a stand of Noble fir trees as a background. The second shot was of Dad and Joey sitting on a huge boulder.

"One more," Mom said. "Stand behind that patch of blue columbine." The shutter clicked, then Mom said the blue columbine was the Colorado State flower. Joey said he wanted to make a note of that in his Scout notebook after they came back from their hike.

"Don't get lost now," Mom called as Joey and Dad turned to go.

Joey shuddered at the thought. Remembering last summer along Red River, he did not want to get lost again, ever.

"I don't think there's much danger," Dad called back to Mom.

"I sure wish I had my compass, though." Joey let Dad take the lead.

"Don't you trust me, son?" Dad said.

"Sure, I trust you. But if I had my compass I could tell which way is north and which way is south." Again, he tried to remember where he had put the compass. Somewhere for safekeeping, he knew, but he could not remember where.

"Think about it this way," Dad said. "The sun rises in the east and sets in the west. When you're facing the rising sun, north is to your left. When you're facing the setting sun, north is to your right."

But Joey had to forget about the compass and left and right and north and south. He had to watch his step. The thick carpet of brown pine needles slipped and slid under his new hiking boots as he climbed the steep mountainside. He stepped on a pine cone, which rolled, and he fell to his all-fours.

"Ouch!" he said, feeling the prickly needles under his bare hands. The dusty smell of the decaying cones and needles made his nose twitch.

"Are you finding the going a bit rough?" Dad asked from higher up.

"I never thought it'd be this hard to climb a mountain," Joey said, scrambling to his feet.

"That's because you're always on level ground at home," Dad said. He stopped suddenly, and Joey bumped into him.

"Look," Dad said. He and Joey stood still and watched two brown-and-tan-striped chipmunks scamper over a log and dart under a rock.

"I wish I had them for pets," Joey said.

Dad laughed. "I'll bet your mother would let you keep all you can catch."

"You mean I can't catch them?" Joey asked.

"Let's just say that I've never been able to catch one." Dad climbed on.

Following close behind, Joey looked as far as he could see in every direction in the deep forest of evergreens. They had lost sight of the cabin almost immediately.

Very little sunshine touched the ground here, but pink and yellow and white flowers pushed up through the dried pine needles. Many kinds of birds sang in the treetops.

Up and up they climbed. Joey thought this mountain must be as high as Pike's Peak. But when they reached the top, they looked across at another mountain much higher. Way down below, a silver ribbon of water twisted and turned and plunged over rocks, making little waterfalls. From this distance, Joey thought, it sounded like the soft rain did on his bedroom window back home.

Joey was hot and tired and thirsty. He'd have liked some of the cookies Mom had packed for their lunch, but he wanted to prove to Dad that he was man enough to go on hikes, so he didn't complain. Back home, when other boys in his Cub Pack had talked about how much fun they'd had on hikes with their dads, Joey had felt left out. He wanted to be able to talk about hikes, too. Also, he wanted to overcome his fear of the forest if he could.

"Dad, the air smells so clean up here," he said.

"It sure does. No pollution up here." Dad started down the mountainside. "Careful now," he warned. "Sometimes it's more dangerous going down than it is climbing up. Oops!" A rock gave way under Dad's foot and went crashing down. Dad slipped and scooted on his bottom some little distance, his backpack bouncing

on the ground behind him.

Joey watched wide-eyed until Dad grabbed a little pine tree and righted himself. Then Joey turned and backed down the steep place, like climbing down a ladder.

"Hey, now, don't tell me you're going to make a better mountain climber than your old dad." Dad grinned, but he looked a little shook up. "Let's rest awhile."

"Okay," Joey said. He, too, felt a bit shaky, but he was glad his father seemed pleased with him. "Mountain climbing is almost as hard as they make it look on television." He sat down on a rock sticking out of the side of the mountain, pushed his cap back, and wiped sweat off his face.

CHAPTER 3

While resting, Joey and Dad listened to bluejays screaming in the treetops above and the rushing of the water below. Soon they began picking their way on down the mountain. They went into forest so thick that it gave Joey a closed-in feeling; the same kind of feeling he'd had last year when he had gotten lost along Red River.

"Dad, are we lost?" The words slipped out.

"Of course not. What makes you think we're lost?"

"Look, Dad. The creek!" Joey shouted as they rounded a fat cedar tree and came out into a more open place. He was glad he didn't have to answer Dad's question about being lost. He didn't want Dad to know how scared he had been. From here, the rushing water sounded more like a hard rain pouring off a housetop.

"I'll race you to the creek," Joey shouted above the sound of the water.

"Wait!" Dad grabbed Joey's backpack.

Joey looked up at his father.

"The banks of mountain streams often change during flood periods," Dad explained. "Three years ago when the fellows and I were here deer hunting, this was a safe place to cross. But it looks different now. It may be dangerous."

The bank directly below them was very steep. No grass or trees grew on it or on the narrow beach between the bank and the rushing water.

"That sand and gravel is going to go right out from under us on that steep bank," Dad said, wiping his face with his handkerchief.

"I can make it if you can," Joey said. He thought it would be fun to slide down the bank.

"Okay," Dad said. "Strike out. Just make sure you don't pitch headlong into the creek."

From where they were, the water didn't look more than inches deep to Joey, and he thought it would be fun to go splashing into it. The bank was so steep it was like going down a ladder face-first. He made deep tracks in the loose sand and gravel as he went, and his seat was scraping the ground most of the time. He used his hands behind him on both sides to slow himself down. Just the same, he gathered so much momentum that he had to put on his brakes good and hard to keep from plunging into the creek. The rushing of the water was so loud that all other forest sounds were shut out.

Joey could see everything in the clear water, from the smallest pieces of gravel to the biggest rocks. Even the hairline brown stripes running through the pink and yellow and gray stones were as plain as pencil lines on paper.

"Wow!" he said as Dad stopped beside him. "Is it safe to drink?"

"The best in the world," Dad said. They lay down on their stomachs and took long drinks.

Joey's lips got so cold they felt numb. He pressed the back of his warm hand against them.

"This is the best water I ever tasted," Joey said. Then he took another long drink.

"It's melted snow," Dad said. "See. It's coming from way up there."

Following Dad's gaze, Joey squinted against the brightness of a snowcapped mountain glistening in the morning sunlight. The sky beyond was a deep blue.

"Wow!" Joey said. "It must be cold up there." He shivered in spite of the warmth of the valley.

As they stood looking up, a big bird lifted off a distant cliff and soared down into the valley.

"Look, Dad!" Joey exclaimed. "A bald eagle!"

"It sure is," Dad said.

"Did you know it's a thousand dollar fine to kill one of those birds?" Joey asked.

"So I've heard," Dad said.

"That's because they're on the endangered species list," Joey explained. The eagle disappeared into the timber, and Joey asked, "Will there be snow at Mason's mine?"

"I'm afraid not." Dad grinned. "We won't be anywhere near that high up."

"I don't think we could climb that high in one day," Joey said.

"I think you're right," Dad agreed. "That peak is many, many miles from here."

Joey looked at the creek and said, "Too bad the water isn't deep enough for fish."

"It's deep enough," Dad assured him. "See that blue hole? That's over your head."

"You're teasing me," Joey said. "I can see rocks on the bottom of that hole."

"Just don't fall in it," Dad said. "Unless you plan to swim like a fish."

Leading the way, Dad picked out the biggest rocks at the shallowest place in the creek and began stepping and jumping from one to the next. Sometimes he stepped in water ankle deep.

Joey stepped in and felt the cold water flow around his boots. Halfway across, he decided to see just how deep the water was; he let one foot slip off a rock to step down to the bottom. His breath came in a sharp gasp as the icy water filled his boot and swirled around his knee. He lost his balance and the other foot went in, too. He was standing in water over his knees when he looked up and saw his father laughing from the far bank.

"What happened, Joey?" Dad called. "Did you fall in?"

Joey sloshed on across.

"You're right, Dad," he said. "That water's lots deeper than it looks." He stood shivering in a warm puddle of sunlight.

CHAPTER 4

Joey liked it better on this side of the creek. The trees were not as thick, and he could see some little distance in most directions. He didn't feel so closed in.

Dad angled along the side of the mountain, gradually climbing higher. The sound of the rushing water grew fainter and fainter. After awhile, they lost all sight and sound of the creek.

"Dad, I'm not afraid as long as I'm with you," Joey said, trying hard not to think about getting lost. "But how do you know we can find our way back?"

"It's simple," Dad said. "We just watch where we're going. Then when we start back we simply retrace our steps."

"But how do you know we'll retrace our steps?"

"See that boulder?" Dad stopped and pointed at a huge rock just ahead of them.

"Yes," Joey said. "But there are lots of boulders that size."

"Right," Dad agreed. "But what's different about that one?"

Joey studied the big rock. "They all look alike to me."

"But this one has a little blue spruce growing at the left side of it," Dad said.

Joey nodded.

"Now," Dad said. "When we start back the little blue spruce will be on our right."

"Left, right." Joey said, trying to remember which was his left hand and which was his right. In his mind he said, *East, west, north, south.* But since he didn't know one from the other he shook his head.

They walked on past the boulder, then Dad turned and said, "See. The blue spruce is on our right."

"Right!" Joey put up his writing hand. Then he turned around and said, "Left, right." But he wasn't the least bit sure he would remember which was which. He hadn't had any trouble—well, not much trouble—learning to tie his shoelaces or telling time, but when it came to directions, Mom said he had a blind spot. Joey wasn't sure what that meant, but, well, he wouldn't worry about it right now. He was with Dad, and Dad wouldn't get lost. He ran to catch up with his father.

They came out into an open space, and again Dad stopped and pointed, this time high above and beyond them.

"What do you see up there?" Dad asked.

Joey looked and looked, wondering what it was his father wanted him to see.

"Nothing," Joey said, "except three tall tree trunks in a row."

"Exactly." Dad sounded pleased. "Now three trees that grew in a straight row is very unusual. You can't find a better landmark than that." Dad walked on, talking as he went.

"Many years ago," Dad said. "there was a forest fire up there, and those big trees were burned so badly they died—but their trunks still stood. The smaller trees around them were burned to the ground. We know it happened a long time ago because young trees are dotting the mountainside again."

Joey wished he could still see the three blackened tree trunks, but they had walked into timber that shut out the view.

"And look at that dead soldier," Dad said. Joey jumped, and Dad laughed. "I mean that fallen tree ahead of us." They walked to the log and studied the twisted, splintered line running from end to end.

"What would you say caused that?" Dad asked.

Joey thought hard and made a wild guess. "Lightning?"

"Right," Dad said. "See. You're not so bad. You'll make a fine woodsman."

Joey's chest swelled. He was losing some of his fear of the forest. He ran on ahead, then, hearing something

crashing in a thicket, he stopped short.

"Joey." Dad called in a hoarse whisper. "Stand still. Don't move. Don't make a sound."

Joey leaned this way and that, peering through the few trees between him and the thicket. Dad crept up behind and laid a hand on Joey's shoulder.

"Don't move," Dad whispered again. They stood very still, listening to the crashing noise in the thicket ahead of them. A big bear walked out and Joey jumped. Dad squeezed hard on Joey's shoulder.

They watched silently, Joey trembling inside, until the bear lumbered down the mountain and lost himself in the deepening forest. Joey let his breath out slowly.

"Dad, we don't even have a gun," he whispered.

"We don't need one." Dad spoke in a normal tone. "He won't bother us if we don't bother him. But I'm glad we were downwind from him."

"Why?" Joey's throat felt tight and his heart thumped.

"Bears are very nearsighted," Dad explained, "but they have a keen sense of smell. If he had smelled our bacon and apples he might have invited himself to lunch."

"I think I'd give him my lunch and run," Joey said, remembering that he was carrying the bacon and apples.

"And I think I'd be right behind you," Dad said, chuckling.

Joey was afraid to run ahead and he was afraid to

walk behind. He let Dad go between himself and the bear, but he kept looking around to see if the bear had turned back. They skirted the thicket some distance uphill from where the bear had been. A little farther on, they came out into an opening in the forest and suddenly faced a big hole in the side of the mountain. Joey stopped short.

"Dad, is that the bear's den?" His voice squeaked.

"No." Dad laughed. "That's Mason's mine."

"Really!" Joey wanted to run ahead to the mine, but he didn't want to, either. Suppose, just suppose, a whole family of bears lived in the old mine?

CHAPTER 5

"Do you think bears live in the mine?" Joey asked.

"What do you say we look for tracks before we go bolting in?" Dad suggested.

"I think that's a good idea," Joey said.

The entrance to the old mine was framed with logs that were rotting and falling down. Dirt had sifted through the cracks, making brown, powdery dust on the ground. Grass grew in the cracks and in the rotting places in the logs. Joey and his father searched the entrance carefully. Dad tried to shake the logs with his hands.

"What do you think?" Joey asked.

"Well, at least there aren't any wild animal tracks in sight," Dad said. "And the logs seem to be steady enough."

They unstrapped their backpacks and fished out their flashlights. Before going inside the mine, they looked all around. Only small trees grew up the mountainside high above the mine entrance. The area up there lay thick with big boulders, and Joey's father said it looked like a fire had been there, too.

"Look! Look!" Joey shouted. "Two deer!"

Dad smiled and nodded. "They're having a good romp up there." The deer disappeared among the little trees and the big rocks, and Dad said, "Shall we go inside?"

"I'll let you go first," Joey said.

Dad gave Joey's cap a knuckle-scrub and went inside the mine. They shone their flashlights in all directions. The walls and ceiling were shored up with logs, and a small train track went beyond the beams of their lights. They moved on cautiously.

Tap, tap, tap, came a sound from nearby.

"Wh-what's that?" Joey whispered.

"Water dripping from the ceiling." Dad's voice sounded spooky. He shone his light on a wet spot on the mine wall, making the wet places look like animal eyes shining in the dark. Dad's light traveled down to a small pool on the mine floor.

"If you'd like to know what gold water tastes like," Dad said, "have a drink."

"Is it safe?" Joey asked.

"Sure. Go ahead and taste it," Dad said.

Joey crept to the pool and shone his light in it. The water was very clear, but it was ringed with a brownish-gold sediment. He looked up at his father.

"It's perfectly safe." Dad squatted down, dipped up a handful of the water, and drank it.

Joey dipped up a handful and tasted it. "Yech!" He flung the water from him, wiped his mouth on his sleeve and his hand on his shirt front.

"Dad! How can you swallow that stuff?" Joey said. "It's bitter, and puckery, and it tastes worse than medicine."

"The old-timers thought it was medicine." Dad grinned at Joey. "Good medicine. Mineral water, they called it. But I grant you, I can live a long time without it."

Then Joey heard a rumbling, thudding noise overhead and far away. Dad heard it, too, and he shouted, "Run, Joey! Run! It's a cave-in!"

Joey wheeled about and ran for the square of daylight at the end of the tunnel. The bumping, thudding noise grew louder with every leap he made. Dad was right behind him, but he yelled, "Stop, Joey! Stop!"

Joey could not stop. For one thing, he was running too fast to stop, and for another, he was too scared to stop. Just as he reached the mouth of the mine, a huge boulder shot off right in front of him and went bouncing on down the mountainside. If Joey had been a split second faster he would have been crushed by the big stone. But he wasn't hurt, and hearing the logs crashing down behind him, he kept running for his life.

He was a long way off when he realized all was quiet. He turned and looked wildly about. Dust hovered at what had been the mine entrance, which was now completely blocked by the fallen logs. Dad was nowhere in sight.

Joey ran back to the mine and found his father lying facedown under a pile of logs. Only his head and hands stuck out.

CHAPTER 6

"Dad! Dad!" Joey screamed and screamed.

Dad's face was in the dirt. He turned his head and moved one arm. "Joey!" he called. "Listen to me!"

"I'll get you out, Dad!" Joey cried. "I'll get you out!" He reached for a log.

"Joey!" Dad yelled. "Don't! Don't touch a thing! Listen to me!"

Joey squeezed his face with both hands and tried to listen to his father. He was shaking all over.

"I'm lying across a log," Dad said. "And there's another log across my back. One end of the top log must be propped up on something because it isn't mashing me too hard. But my feet and legs are tangled in more logs. If you move anything you might make the whole mess start shifting. My back could be broken, or I could be crushed to death. Do you understand, Joey?"

Too scared to speak, Joey nodded. He felt hot tears running down his face.

"Sit down here by me, son," Dad said. "Be careful. Don't touch a log."

Joey sat down and Dad took one of his hands. "Listen to me, son. You have to go for help."

Joey's teeth chattered. "But, Dad, I . . . I'm afraid. You know how I get l-lost in the woods."

"You won't get lost, son," Dad said. "You won't get lost. And you have to go."

"B-but . . . the bear! I'm afraid of the bear." Joey tried to keep from screaming and crying. Dad held his hand tightly.

"Son, I'm afraid, too," Dad said. "I'm afraid I can't stay here this way very long. And I'm afraid to move for fear the logs will shift and crush me. The only way you can help me is by going for help. Now listen to me." Dad patted Joey's hand.

Joey trembled, but he tried to listen.

"Go to the cabin," Dad said. "Tell your mother to go to the forest ranger station. She knows where it is. Tell her to have the forest ranger send a rescue party for me. They'll know where Mason's mine is." Dad looked at his watch. "It's eleven o'clock. If you hurry you'll probably find your mother eating her lunch."

Joey wanted to go, but he felt frozen to the ground.

"What is your Cub motto, son?" Dad asked, squeezing Joey's hand hard.

"Do your best." Joey squeezed the words out.

"That's all Daddy's asking you to do." Dad gave him a gentle swat on the leg. "Now go."

Joey jumped up and ran.

"Joey," Dad called.

"Yes, Dad?" Joey stopped and looked over his shoulder.

"Daddy loves you."

"I love you, too." Tears streamed down Joey's face as he ran.

Dashing the tears away with first one fist then the other, Joey ran and ran. He only glanced toward the thicket where they had seen the bear. His feet slipped and slid, but he was running so fast that he never quite fell down. Small rocks dislodged under his boots and rolled down the mountainside. Joey kept on running. Dad had to have help.

Joey's chest began to ache. His stomach hurt. Every time a foot hit the ground it felt like a hammer hit inside his head. He got a stitch in his side, and he had to slow down. He could hardly breathe.

But Dad was lying under a pile of logs, and Joey knew it was hard for him to breathe, too. He hoped no more logs caved in. He hoped those that were on Dad did not start to roll. He started running fast again, running with all his might. Once, he caught sight of an animal bolting through the timber, but he didn't stop to see what it was.

At the creek, he sloshed across, not even trying to stay

on the higher rocks. When he leaped out on the other side he was soaked to his waist. He crossed the narrow beach with a single bound and tried to climb the steep bank where he and Dad had made the deep tracks on their way over. But the loose sand and gravel kept shifting so that he could not get a footing. Every step sent him to his knees, then to his stomach. He scratched and clawed and tried with all his might to crawl up the slope on his hands and knees. He simply could not.

Panting and sobbing, he allowed himself to slide down onto the narrow beach. He was covered with sand and gravel, and the stuff scraped his legs inside his boot tops. His lungs begged for air. His legs jerked, and his hands were raw from clawing at the loose, coarse gravel.

"If only I wasn't so tired," he sobbed. "I know I could make it if I wasn't so tired."

After awhile he rolled over and washed his face and hands in the icy water. Then he took a good drink.

"Oh, Dad," he cried aloud. "I know you'd like to have a drink, too."

Slowly, Joey pushed himself to a sitting position. He studied the creek bank from both directions. Immediately upstream, the creek fanned out wide and flowed against a sheer rock face on this side. It would be impossible to climb up there.

He looked downstream. The bank above the blue hole of water that Dad had said was over Joey's head was not as steep as it was here, but it dropped into the water without any beach at all. If Joey should try to climb up at that point, and if he should slip, he'd plunge into the deep hole. This, he thought, was no time to swim like a fish. He bit his lip, but his chin trembled just the same.

CHAPTER 7

Joey looked up the mountainside. If only he could make it up to that rock where he had sat down for a few minutes this morning when he and Dad had come over the mountain. He got to his feet and rubbed both legs, trying to stop the jerking.

Again, he studied the bank above the blue hole of water. Rocks and seedling aspens and evergreen trees dotted the slope up the mountainside. Joey did not know whether the little trees would hold his weight or not. Remembering the rock that had given way under his dad's feet this morning and the huge boulder that had come tumbling down the mountain, causing the mine cave-in, he was afraid to trust the rocks.

He got down on his hands and knees and climbed high enough to take hold of the first little aspen with both hands. Then testing a rock with one foot to see if it would stay put, he pulled with all his might. The aspen didn't budge, so he climbed higher and grasped a little cedar tree. "Ouch!" It was very stickery to his skinned hands. But it held, and that was the important thing.

Cautiously, rock by rock and little tree by little tree, Joey climbed to where he could stand upright. Then he hurried as fast as he could go. He was so tired by the time he reached the top of the mountain that he fell down on the ground and breathed hard. His chest felt like it was being crushed. He hoped Dad wasn't being crushed by the logs. He staggered to his feet and ran down the mountainside, his knees threatening to buckle under him with every step.

The instant he caught sight of the cabin he began screaming, "Mom! Mom!" He burst in at the back door. "Mom! Mom!" But Mom was not there. The station wagon was gone, too. Joey looked about, his heart pounding.

"Mom! Where are you?" he screamed. Then he saw a note propped against a bowl of wild flowers on the kitchen table. He grabbed it and read through blinding tears and fear:

Dear boys,

Just in case you beat me home, I have gone to Colorado Springs for groceries. If anything is showing that I want to see, I just might stay for a movie.

Love,
Mom

"Oh, no!" Joey screamed. He dropped onto a chair, pounded the table with his fists and cried hard. *What could he do?* It was miles and miles to Colorado Springs, and he did not know where the ranger station was. He tried to think.

The cabin sat some little distance back from the gravel road, which Joey figured few people ever traveled. But maybe, just maybe, somebody would come along.

He ran out the door and down the bumpy lane that led to the gravel road. He looked and listened and would have started running again except that he didn't know which way to go. His heart gave a leap when he heard a truck motor.

Joey waited until the truck turned the bend uphill from him. It was a huge truck, and it was loaded high with the biggest logs he had ever seen. The driver

pressed the horn, which shot a deafening blast through the mountains. Joey jumped to the side of the road and began waving his arms and screaming, "Help! Help!"

The downhill grade was very steep, and the driver busied himself with the grinding gears of his truck. The thing passed Joey so fast and so close that the wind from it nearly knocked him down. In that instant, he was as scared for himself as he was for Dad. He stood there, staring after the truck until the long, long logs went out of sight around a sharp bend in the steep road. Dust boiled up behind it.

Before Joey could collect himself, he heard another motor. Wheeling about, he saw another truck just like the first one coming around the bend above him. He jumped farther back from the road and again waved his arms and shouted, "Help! Help!"

The driver hit his horn, ground his gears, and went careening down the mountainside, his red flag snapping in the wind at the end of the long, long logs.

Joey threw himself down and pounded the ground with both fists. "Somebody's got to help me!" he cried. But nobody heard. Exhausted, he lay there a long time, breathing hard.

He listened, sat up, and listened closely. Yes, it was. Another motor. He sprang to his feet in time to see a red Volkswagen round the bend above him. In a split second, he decided to take no chances on this one getting away. He ran to the middle of the road and jumped up and down, waving his arms and screaming, *"Help! Help! You've got to help me!"*

The driver hit the horn, but Joey refused to get out of the road. *"Help! Help!"* he yelled. The driver stomped on the brakes and the Volkswagen jumped out of the road and back in again. A red blur was coming straight at Joey. He shut his eyes and braced himself.

CHAPTER 8

Joey opened his eyes wide and laid both hands on the front of the red Volkswagen. He was too scared to move. Two boys who looked to be in their teens jumped out of the car. They grabbed hold of Joey on both sides and nearly shook his teeth out.

"You little brat!" the driver shouted, shaking his blond hair out of his face. "Why did you do that?"

"Somebody's got to help me!" Joey shouted back.

"I ought to help him break your stinking little neck," said the other boy. He wore a dark beard, and he looked hard at Joey with his dark eyes.

"What if my brakes hadn't held? I would have broken every bone in your body!" The driver's blue eyes snapped.

"My dad's under a pile of logs and maybe every bone in his body's already broken," Joey screamed.

"What? Where?" the boys asked.

"In Mason's mine." Joey's voice trembled.

The two older boys looked at each other. "I never heard of Mason's mine," said the one with the beard.

"Neither have I," said the blond boy.

"I can take you to it," Joey said. "No, no! I mean, Dad said take me to the forest ranger station. Do you know where it is?"

"We know where the ranger station is," said the one with the beard, "but how do we know you're telling us the truth?"

"A Cub Scout doesn't lie," Joey said, standing tall. "Besides, I wouldn't jump in front of a car if I didn't need help."

"Where's your mother?" asked the one with the beard.

"She went to town," Joey said. "She left a note."

"Get in the car," the driver said. "I believe you, but you scared the living daylights out of me."

Joey sat between the older boys. The blond turned the car around and roared up the hill. He turned at the second corner and drove down a very rough road. Joey was so glad finally to be headed for the ranger station that he paid no attention to which way they went. He tried to relax, but he was still breathing very hard when the driver jabbed him with his elbow.

"I still want to know why you jumped in front of my car and just stood there," he demanded.

"Because two logging trucks had already passed me by. I had to have help, and I didn't want you to leave me standing there by the side of the road like they did." Joey felt his chin trembling.

The boys whistled low.

"Kid, if you had jumped in front of one of those logging trucks, you'd be bug dust by now," said the one with the beard. He gave Joey a hard squeeze.

"I know." Joey felt cold, and he shook like a leaf.

They started up a steep grade, and there on top of a high point stood the ranger station. Joey's heart pounded hard. As soon as the car stopped, he jumped out behind the bearded boy and ran up the station steps.

"Whoa there." A pretty young woman grabbed Joey by the shoulders. "What can I do for you?"

Jerking loose from her, Joey demanded, "Where's the forest ranger?"

She smiled and asked, "What would you say if I told you I'm the forest ranger?"

Joey gulped. But he didn't have time for games. "My dad!" he screamed. "Mason's mine caved in on him!"

"What?" Her eyes grew big and round.

"Dad said send a rescue squad. He's way over . . . " Joey was so mixed up that he did not know which way the mine was.

The forest ranger looked at the boys, who had climbed to the top of the station behind Joey. They nodded, and she said, "Never mind. We know where the old mine is." She reached for the telephone.

"Burt, this is Dolly," the ranger said into the telephone. "We have a man trapped in Mason's old abandoned mine. . . . Yes . . . Right." She turned to Joey and asked, "What's your name, Scout?"

"Joey Johnson. My dad is Joe Johnson. He's crushed under the logs."

The boy with the beard said, "His mother has gone to Colorado Springs."

"Burt, you'd better send a helicopter ambulance," the forest ranger said into the phone. "Colorado Springs . . . Right. General Hospital . . . Okay."

Joey sank to the floor and closed his eyes. He had never been so tired in all his life. Thank goodness, Dad would get help. And a helicopter would be lots faster than going in on foot. Joey heard the others talking, but their words seemed to float over his head.

"Come on, Joey," one of the boys said. "We'll take you back to the cabin."

Joey stumbled down the steps, holding the rail with both hands.

At the cabin, the two older boys got out of the Volkswagen and went inside with Joey. Mom still wasn't home. Joey thought the boys acted nervous about something.

"Look, pal," the blond boy said. "You've been a real Cub Scout hero today, and I just know you'll earn an achievement for it, but are you afraid to stay by yourself till your mother gets here?"

Joey hadn't even thought about an achievement, and he had no idea when his mother would be back.

"I'm not afraid," he said. "But don't you think I ought to go and stay with Dad till the helicopter gets there?"

"No. Don't do that," the blond boy said quickly. "I figure the helicopter is already there. They'll be gone with your dad before you can get there."

"Remember what the forest ranger told you?" asked the one with the beard.

"W-what did he tell me?" Joey asked, frowning.

"I think he was too scared and too tired to hear much of anything," the blond boy said.

Joey looked at the floor and nodded.

"*She* said to tell your mother to go to General Hospital," the boy said. "Because that's where they'll take your dad."

"General Hospital," Joey repeated the name. "Yes, I remember now. That's what the forest ranger said. But he was a she."

The older boys laughed.

"You won't forget?" asked the blond boy.

"No, I won't forget," Joey said.

"We really ought to go," he said. "You see, we were on our way back to work after lunch. We're late now. We've had this job only two days and we'd hate to get fired."

So that was why they were acting nervous, Joey thought.

"You're a good Scout, Joey," said the one with the beard. "We're sorry we got rough with you." He ruffled Joey's hair. "You won't leave the cabin till your mother gets here?"

"No, I won't leave," Joey promised. He lifted one hand to wave good-bye. "Thanks for helping me. I'm sorry I stopped in front of your car and scared you."

"That's all right, Scout." The blond boy winked and grinned. "Just don't ever risk it again."

"I won't," Joey said. "And I hope you don't get fired."

The boys left, and Joey went to the kitchen and read his mother's note again. There was no hint of when she might get home.

Joey felt lonely, and very empty. Not hungry, just empty. But he was not afraid. At least, not for himself. He hoped the helicopter ambulance was on its way to General Hospital with Dad by now. If only there hadn't been more cave-ins. . . . He wished Mom would come home.

CHAPTER 9

Joey's hiking boots felt full of gravel. Finding a clean pair of socks and sneakers, he went out and sat down on the front steps where he took off his boots and brushed the sand and gravel off his feet and legs. The cool air felt good to his chafed skin. He was sitting there wiggling his toes when the yellow station wagon turned into the narrow road leading up to the cabin.

"Mom!" he yelled. Socks and sneakers in hand, he ran to meet his mother. "Mom! Don't even stop!"

But Mom did stop the station wagon, and Joey ran around and jumped in beside her.

"General Hospital," he said. "We have to go to General Hospital!"

"Joey," Mom said. "What has come over you?"

"Dad! They're taking him to General Hospital in a helicopter ambulance."

"But why?"

"Mason's mine caved in on Dad. Mom, don't stop the car. He may be dead!" Joey hadn't meant to say that.

Mom shut off the motor, shook Joey, and felt his forehead.

"Joey, will you please calm down and tell me what has happened?" she said.

"I just told you!" Tears streamed down Joey's face. "The mine caved in. Dad was all covered with logs and he sent me for help and you weren't here and two boys took me to the forest ranger station but they had to go on to work, and, Mom, the forest ranger is a girl and she said for you and me to meet Dad at General Hospital in Colorado Springs because that's where the helicopter ambulance would take him." Joey was out of breath, but Mom got the message.

She started the station wagon, backed out into the gravel road, and turned toward Colorado Springs. Joey put his socks and shoes on as fast as his hands would fly.

Mom stopped in the parking lot, and Joey had to run to keep up with her. Inside the hospital, she stopped at the information desk.

"Emergency," Mom said to the woman sitting behind the desk. "Would you please show me to emergency?"

"Exactly what do you want?" the woman asked. She didn't act the least bit excited.

"It's about Joe Johnson," Mom said. "A mine caved in on him, and they were to bring him here."

"In a helicopter ambulance," Joey said.

"Oh, yes," the woman said. "Down this way to the second door, then to your left for two more doors and to your right . . ."

Left, right, north, south, Joey thought, shaking his head.

Mom grabbed his hand and away they went down the long halls. They stopped at another desk where they were told, Yes, a Joe Johnson had been admitted, but no one was allowed in emergency.

"But I must see him," Mom said. "He's my husband."

"Please have seats," the woman said. "We'll let you know as soon as word comes to the desk."

Mom stood there a moment, then she and Joey found a big, empty chair and huddled close in it. Other people were sitting in other chairs. While they waited, Joey told Mom more of the exciting details of the day.

Occasionally, Mom said, "And then what did you do?" or "What happened next?" But she scarcely ever took her eyes off the desk.

"I was leading the way," Joey said, "and I heard something in a thicket and out walked this big, black bear."

"What?" Mom nearly jumped out of the chair. Other people turned to look at them, and Mom said in a quieter tone, "What did you say, Joey?"

"Sure enough, Mom," Joey said. "It was the biggest bear I ever saw."

"You mean your father was lying up there under a pile of logs with a bear nearby?" Mom's blue eyes held a frightened look.

"Yes. And Dad said if the bear smelled our bacon and apples he might invite himself to lunch," Joey said.

"Oh, dear." Mom put one hand over her mouth. Joey could feel her trembling.

"Maybe the bear didn't come back," Joey said, hoping to make his mother feel better.

He looked up and saw Dad coming in a wheelchair. One leg was in a cast, and it was sticking straight out in front of him. Mom saw, too, and they both jumped up at the same time. Dad wore a big, broad grin.

"Son, you did it," Dad said when Joey ran to him. Mom came up on the other side of the wheelchair.

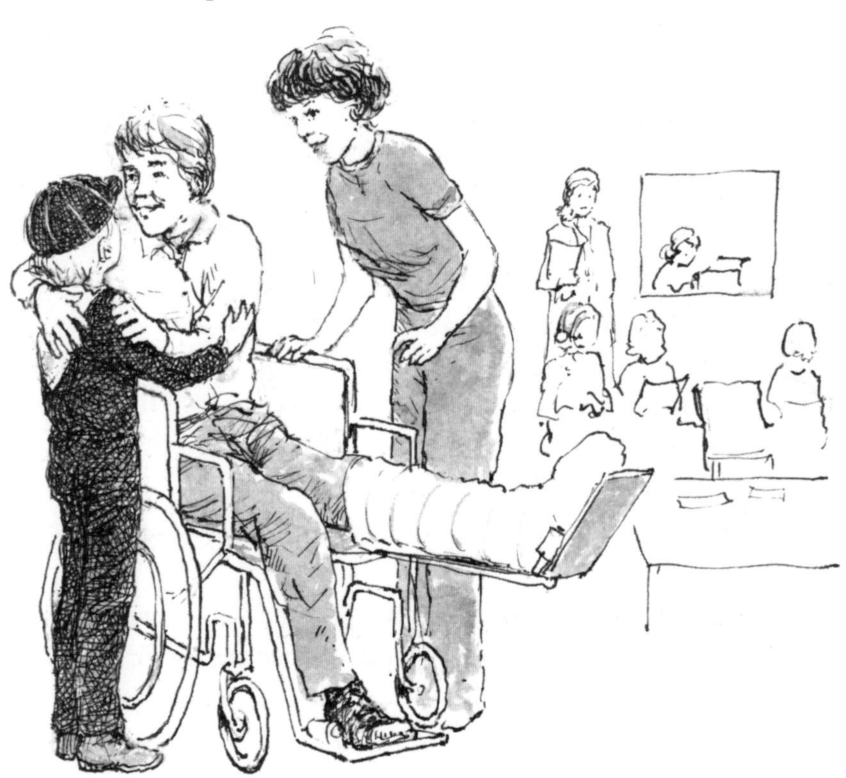

"Joe. Oh, Joe," Mom said, hugging Dad.

Dad kissed Mom, then he squeezed Joey hard, saying, "So you really rescued your old dad. I knew you'd do it."

Joey's Cub Scout uniform was a rumpled mess, and he had left his cap at the cabin, but he felt as proud as a peacock.

The man pushing the wheelchair had stopped to let the family visit a minute.

"So you're the hero I've been hearing about," he said, smiling broadly at Joey. "I'll bet you'll be glad to have these back, too." He pointed to Dad's and Joey's backpacks on the little cart at the back of the wheelchair.

"Oh, boy! Yes, sir, I sure am," Joey said. "I'm sure glad the rescuers remembered to bring them."

In a matter of minutes, Dad was settled in the back seat of the station wagon with his left leg sticking straight out on the seat. Somebody had ripped his pant leg all the way down so the cast would go through. The man pushing the wheelchair put the backpacks in the car. Joey and Mom climbed into the front seat.

"Take good care of him, now." The man waved and turned back to the hospital.

Joey stood on the seat on his knees so he could look at his father. "Dad, I sure am glad it's your left leg. That way, it won't keep you from driving when you feel like it."

"But, Joey, I thought you didn't know left from right," Mom said as she pulled out of the parking lot.

"Well, I know that Dad uses his right foot on the gas pedal," Joey said. "So I guess that makes the other one his left foot."

"Right." Mom gave him a love swat on the seat of his pants.

"Right. Left." Joey put up first one fist, then the other. "I bet I don't ever forget which is which again."

Dad reached out and took Joey's head between his hands and gave it a good squeeze. "Thanks, old man," he said, coughing a little.

"Really, Joe, how badly are you hurt?" Mom asked.

"Not near as badly as I might have been," Dad said. "Only one little ol' bone in the side of my foot is broken." He coughed again, then added, "Of course, I've got a couple of fractured ribs. They've got me taped so tight I can hardly breathe." *Cough, cough.*

Looking worried, Mom pulled to the far right and slowed the car. "Don't you think you should have stayed in the hospital?" she asked.

"No!" Dad exclaimed. "Who wants to spend their vacation in a hospital?"

"Then at least stop talking," Mom said. "Because if you develop a bad cough and start running a fever, I'm taking you right back." She picked her way through the traffic.

"Joey, sit down and fasten your seatbelt," she said, "so I can drive without throwing you all over the car."

Joey did as Mom said, but he kept stretching up to look back over the seat at his father.

"We're sure lucky to have you alive, Dad," he said.

CHAPTER
10

Dad refused to go to bed, so Mom made him comfortable on the couch in the front room. Joey brought a pillow for Dad's head.

"Thanks, son." Dad put an arm around Joey. "You're the one we're lucky to have alive."

"What do you mean?" Mom said, looking from Dad to Joey.

"I mean, if that boulder had hit him . . ." Dad closed his eyes and squeezed Joey hard.

"What boulder?" Mom asked. "Joe, what are you talking about?"

"The cave-in was caused by a dislodged boulder," Dad said. "When I first heard the rumbling, I told Joey to run. But then when I heard the boulder bouncing down the mountain overhead, I yelled at him to stop. But he was running too fast to stop, and the thing shot off right over his head." Dad squinted his eyes and squeezed Joey again.

Mom turned pale, and Joey thought she was going to faint.

"But I'm all right," he said, putting up both hands.

"You sure are," Dad said. "In more ways than one. And I'll be all right, too. Just you wait and see. After a couple of nights, I'll be able to sleep in that pup tent with you." He tousled Joey's hair. "Of course, I won't be able to cook our breakfast. You'll have to do that."

"Oh, boy," Joey said. "And I'll get to earn another achievement."

"And another thing," Dad said. "In a few days, we'll all three take our lunch and drive down to where the road crosses the creek and from there we'll go trout fishing. I'll only need a crooked stick for a walking cane."

Dad and Joey laughed, but Mom shook her head. She started to the kitchen, then turned back.

"My stars," she said. "I forgot all about the groceries. Joey, come and help me bring them in."

Joey helped his mother with the groceries, then he brought the backpacks inside the cabin.

"Hey, look, Dad," he said, rummaging in his pack. "They even picked up our flashlights."

"Those fellows didn't miss a thing, did they?" Dad said.

The smell of the apples reminded Joey that he hadn't eaten since breakfast.

"I'm hungrier than that bear was," he said. "I think I'll take an apple and some cookies and go sit outside awhile."

"That's a good idea," Mom said. "That should tide you over till I get supper ready."

Joey went out the back door, sat down on a log, and listened to birds singing in the treetops. He tossed some cookie crumbs on the ground, but it wasn't birds that came to get them. It was chipmunks. Joey was delighted. The sleek little animals snatched up crumbs and sat on their haunches and nibbled. Joey ran here and there trying to catch one, but they scampered under rocks and brush. He couldn't even get close to one.

Soon he gave up trying to catch a chipmunk and sat down on the log to watch them. When he had eaten all but the apple core, he leaned over and held it out. One chipmunk came close, then darted away. Soon it was back, only to dart away again.

Joey sat very still for a long time. His patience paid off. The furry little creature became bold enough to come up and snatch the apple core out of his hand. Joey smiled. But he did not try to catch the chipmunk. It was enough to have it trust him this far.

He sat on the log a long time, enjoying the cool mountain air. It smelled pure and clean. Birds twittered overhead, and the chipmunks still played about. The forest was filled with sounds strange to Joey, but they were friendly sounds, and he could see why a hike in the

woods was the dream of every Cub Scout. He had been here only one day, but he was beginning to like these tree-covered mountains a lot.

"Joey," Mom called from the back door. "Let's eat."

"I have to go now," Joey said to the chipmunks and the birds. "But I'll be back tomorrow, and I'll bring you lots more to eat."

behind him, and turned to face his parents.

"For the life of me," Mom was saying, "I can't remember whether I stopped the paper or not."

"You stopped it," Joey said. "I heard you talking to Mike on the phone, and I saw you mark it off your list of things to do."

"Good for you." Mom looked relieved.

"But I know how you feel when you can't remember something," Joey said. "I couldn't remember where I put my compass, either. But look what I found." He held out the compass.

"Oh, Joey," Mom said. "Where did you find it?"

"In my project box. I remember putting it there so I wouldn't forget to bring it."

Mom and Dad and Joey laughed.

"But, Dad, you were right," Joey said. "I do have a good compass in my head. I came straight to the cabin from the mine. Without even thinking about it."

"Son, you are all right," Dad said. "I mean, *you are all right.*"

Joey ran outside with his compass, studied it a while, and pointed. "*That* way is north!" he said triumphantly.

After supper, Joey sat out on the front steps and looked at the forest across the road. The sun had dropped behind the mountain west of the cabin, but it was still shining on a higher peak to the east.

Thinking to get his piece of rope and start practicing knots, he went inside and dug into his project box. A shiny object winked up at him. He snatched it up, held it